America's First Railroads

Tim McNeese

Crestwood House
New York

Maxwell Macmillan Canada
Toronto

Maxwell Macmillan International
New York   Oxford   Singapore   Sydney

Design and production: Deborah Fillion
Illustrations: © Chris Duke

Crestwood House
Macmillan Publishing Company
866 Third Avenue
New York, NY 10022

Maxwell Macmillan Canada, Inc.
1200 Eglinton Avenue East
Suite 200
Don Mills, Ontario M3C 3N1

Macmillan Publishing Company is part of the
Maxwell Communication Group of Companies.

First edition

Printed in the United States of America

10 9 8 7 6 5 4 3 2 1

Library of Congress Cataloging-in-Publication Data

McNeese, Tim.
    America's first railroads / by Tim McNeese. —1st ed.
        p.   cm. — (Americans on the move)
    Summary: A history of railroads in the American West.
    ISBN 0-89686-729-3
      1. Railroads—United States—History—Juvenile literature. [1. Railroads.]
I. Title. II. Series: McNeese, Tim. Americans on the move.
TF23.M36 1993
385'.0978—dc20
                                        91-738

Contents

★

Early railroad systems opened up a whole new world to American settlers.

★

Introduction

Every day around the world thousands of trains rush along hundreds of thousands of miles of steel track. Some **locomotives** pull long trains loaded with anything from coal to automobiles to telephone poles to bananas fresh from South America. Others carry thousands of passengers from place to place.

All these trains do a job that no other type of transportation can do. Only gigantic ships can carry as much cargo as trains. Only airplanes can travel faster. But trains are the fastest way to get many tons of freight and passengers to their destinations.

Trains go just about everyplace where there are people. Almost every country in the world has at least one rail system. There are so many railroads around the globe that if all the tracks were put together into one long line they would extend about 800,000 miles. The tracks would stretch from the earth to the moon three times with enough track left over to stretch around the earth at the equator twice!

But all these railroads did not come about in a short period of time. Railroads have been around for almost 200 years. The first railroads using **steam engines** were built in England. But early on, Americans were also experimenting with steam engines. The first American railroads were built during the early decades of the 1800s.

*The Orukter Amphibole
built by Oliver Evans*

The Beginning of the Dream

One of the first men in America to dream of running railroads on steam power was Oliver Evans of Delaware. In 1772, when Evans was 17, he read about a steam engine invented by James Watt, a Scottish engineer. Evans was so fascinated with the idea of creating a steam-powered locomotive that he spent the rest of his life writing about the subject. He also experimented with his own steam engine designs.

During the 1780s and 1790s Evans worked on creating a carriage that would run on steam. He spent all the money he had, living very poorly, trying to design a "steam carriage" that would be practical to build. He finally built a steam-operated dredge that would dig out harbors and riverbeds. He named it the Orukter Amphibole. Evans drove the steam-powered machine from his shop in Philadelphia to the Schuylkill River. However, that was as far as Evans's work on steam carriages took him.

But he never stopped dreaming and writing about a steam engine railroad. In 1813 he wrote about building a railroad from Philadelphia to New York City. No one had ever suggested such an idea before. Evans dreamed about steam engines that could pull cars carrying manufactured goods, farm produce and even passengers. He imagined that the carriages would run on rails that had been set on posts. These rails would guide the carriages. Evans went so far as to dream that steam carriages, guided by such rails, could even run at night. He wrote that steam carriages would travel faster than any other type of transportation: 15 miles an hour, 300 miles a day. Even the fastest stagecoaches of the day only went half that speed! But very few people listened to Oliver Evans. In 1819 Evans died. Until the end of his life he continued to believe that railroad travel would be the transportation of the future.

John Stevens of Hoboken, New Jersey, shared Evans's dream. In the early 1800s Stevens got a **charter**, or written permission, from the state of New Jersey to build a railroad across the state. Stevens later received another charter to build a railroad from Philadelphia west to the Susquehanna River. But Stevens could not get enough rich people to put up money for construction. He did, however, produce so much interest in the idea of building a railroad that some people did start considering the possibilities. They sent a man named William Strickland to England to find out all he could about how to build a railroad.

In 1826 Strickland came back to the United States and reported on what he had learned. He told his fellow

Americans that railroads would be better to build than canals. At that time many Americans thought canals were the best way to move goods. Because of men like Strickland, more people began to think seriously about the future of railroads in the United States.

While Strickland was off in England learning about railroads, Stevens, by then an old man, had designed and built a railroad himself. Built on his own property, the railroad was a circular track with a steam locomotive that Stevens had constructed. He invited people to come and see his steam-powered carriages running on rails. This backyard railroad featured the first locomotive in America to run on a track.

By 1828 the work of dreamers like Evans and Stevens was becoming reality. That year the Baltimore and Ohio Railroad was chartered, and less than a year later, workers began building one of the first important railroads in the United States.

The Baltimore and Ohio Railroad

On the Fourth of July 1828, the city leaders of Baltimore began construction of the Baltimore and Ohio Railroad (B & O). A fine ceremony marked the occasion. The company invited Charles Carroll—the only surviving signer of the Declaration of Independence—to lay a stone. The stone would mark the place where workers would plant the first shovel to build the railroad.

This was not the first railroad in the country, but it was the most elaborately planned railroad at that time. The goal was for the B & O to one day pass through the Appalachian Mountains and extend into the Ohio Valley.

Two years later the first few miles of the B & O were opened. In 1842 the line reached Cumberland, Maryland. Ten years later the line ran all the way to Wheeling, West

Virginia. But railroads were changing and growing very quickly by then. In just four more years, by 1856, the B & O stretched across the eastern half of the United States as far west as St. Louis.

The B & O soon became one of the most important rail lines in the United States. Many of the early improvements in railroading were the result of development by the B & O. The B & O was one of the first lines to use the telegraph. In 1851 the B & O introduced the first electric locomotive.

By that same year the B & O had grown so large that 5,000 men and 1,250 horses were used on the line. The monthly payroll for the railroad was $200,000. The rail line invented new ways to build bridges and dig tunnels. One B & O man, Wendell Bollman, served as the railway's most important bridge builder. Another man, named John Elgar, invented **turntables** and new **switches** for the tracks.

The Little Engine That Could

Interestingly, the B & O did not begin as a steam railroad. Horses were used at first to pull carriages along wooden rails. The age of steam, however, was just around the corner for the railroad line.

In 1830 Peter Cooper, a manufacturer from New York, wanted to convince the owners of the B & O that steam locomotives would do a better job than horses. He was sure steam power would be faster and more reliable. He soon got his chance to prove his theory. The owner of a stagecoach line challenged him to a race between a stagecoach horse and Cooper's steam locomotive, called the Tom Thumb. Cooper eagerly accepted the challenge.

On August 28, 1830, the race was held on a length of double track outside Baltimore. Cooper's engine ran

★

*The first electric locomotive was
introduced by the B & O in 1851.*

★

The famous race of 1830 between the Tom Thumb and a horse-pulled carriage convinced the owners of the B & O to switch to steam locomotives.

against a specially picked horse that pulled a railcar. The railroad locomotive would have won the race if it had not slipped an engine belt. Then the horse was able to pull ahead and win. But by that time B & O officials were convinced that steam power was faster. The day of the rail horse would soon come to an end. And the Tom Thumb was about to make a name for itself as the first American-built steam locomotive to operate on a common carrier rail line. A common carrier transports people, goods or messages for a fee. In service for the B & O the Tom Thumb would pull one of the first passenger trains.

★

Another Contest on the B & O

In need of good locomotives, the B & O held another contest, inviting anyone with a steam locomotive to try their engine on the tracks of the B & O. Phineas Davis, from Grafton County, New Hampshire, loaded his steam engine, the York, into a wagon and hauled it south to Baltimore. One of five entries, the York won the contest. Davis received a prize of $4,000. He was offered a job with the B & O, which he accepted. Davis worked as the manager of the B & O **machine shops** until 1835, when he was killed in an accident. A new locomotive, which he had designed, derailed, and Davis was crushed to death.

★

This steam engine was designed by Phineas Davis for the B & O Railroad.

Others Get
Their Starts

The B & O Railroad was not the only line being built in the early part of the 19th century. By the 1830s railroad building had exploded. Nearly every state east of the Appalachians wanted to get into the railroad business. In South Carolina work began on the Charleston and Hamburg line. It ran within the state from Charleston to the Savannah River bordering Georgia.

In Pennsylvania, after state leaders read the Strickland report about the future of railroading, they were reminded of John Stevens's charter and made plans for rail construction. From Albany, the capital of New York State, a group of investors planned the Mohawk and Hudson line, running west from Albany to Schenectady to connect with the newly constructed Erie Canal. In Virginia the Chesterfield Railroad received a state charter and began laying 13 miles of track from the Falling Creek coal mines to Richmond, the state capital. Lines in other states, including

★

Massachusetts and Delaware, were soon underway, either in planning stages or actually being constructed.

Early Days on the C & H

As important as the B & O Railroad was, this pioneer line was not the first to feature steam-powered locomotives. As we've seen, the B & O had to be convinced to give up horses for steam. It was the Charleston and Hamburg line that made the first run of a steam-powered train in the United States. Its locomotive, called the Best Friend of Charleston, was built at the West Point Foundry of New York. It made the Charleston and Hamburg the first true American railroad. But for all its importance, the C & H line was only six miles long.

The C & H Railroad was formally opened in January 1831. During the celebration, more than 200 people rode the six miles of track. They traveled at the amazing speed of 21 miles per hour. It was certainly faster than other means of overland travel, such as horse or stagecoach. A small cannon was placed on one of the carriages pulled by the Best Friend, and the gun was fired several times along the track.

Not only did the Charleston line feature the first steam locomotive to pull carriages in America, but the line also made history for having the first explosion on a locomotive. The accident happened on June 17, 1831, six months after the official opening of the C & H. A railroad fireman was annoyed by the noise made by escaping steam from the **safety valve** on the Best Friend. So he sat down on the valve lever. But the quiet he produced was soon broken. The **steam boiler** blew up, flew through the air and landed some distance from the engine. The fireman and four others were injured. This explosion naturally kept some people from riding on the C & H for a long time.

★

The explosion of the Best Friend raised concern about the safety of railroads in the 1800s.

After the explosion on the Best Friend, the C & H introduced the "**barrier car**." It was a flatcar piled high with cotton bales. The car was placed between the steam locomotive and the passenger carriages. The idea was that if a steam engine blew up, the pile of cotton bales would protect the passengers from flying debris. This plan did help make the people of Charleston feel better about riding the railway.

Problems with the Early Railways

Early railways like the C & H and the B & O were, by today's standards, inefficient, unsafe and primitive. Most used carriages modeled after stagecoach bodies. They were too top-heavy to ride comfortably on rails. These carriages were soon replaced by flatter-looking cars, more like farm wagons. Over the early years of railroading, these cars were made longer and enclosed with walls, a roof and windows.

Locomotives on these early rail lines were very different from one another. Often the locomotives were nothing more than a flatcar with a boiler sitting on them. The engineer had to stand up on the locomotive platform. And all the early engines left the crew exposed to the weather and the sparks and smoke from the steam engine. A large container, called a tender, was often connected to the engine. It carried the wood for fuel, plus a large barrel of water.

The new railroads were often not very safe. One of the earliest fatal railroad accidents took place in Ohio on the Columbia Railroad in October 1836. A woman named Gibson and her child were killed when an axle on their train car broke. The car dropped down on the track while the train was in motion.

Not only did steam engines explode and carriages

fall apart, but the rails themselves were dangerous. Nearly all early trains carried a sledgehammer that was used when a rail broke. Early rails were strapped (not spiked) onto wooden **ties**. Sometimes the straps broke and a loose rail would crash through the bottom of a carriage floor, injuring passengers. The brakeman or conductor would then take the sledgehammer and knock the loose rail back through the hole in the floor. These broken rail ends were often called "**snake heads**."

Other accidents occurred through the decade of the 1830s. A train on the Boston and Providence Railroad suffered a serious accident on June 21, 1837. One of the train's cars broke an axle, and its load of lumber and shingles toppled onto the passengers in the next car. Two people were killed. In July 1839 a train on the New York and Harlem line, which ran through New York City, jumped off the tracks at Union Park. This accident was bad enough. But while the passengers and crew were working to get the engine back on the track, the boiler blew up, killing several people, including the chief engineer.

By 1840 enough accidents had occurred for someone to question railroad safety. In that year S. A. Howland wrote *Steamboat Disasters and Rail-Road Accidents in the United States*. The book outlined many of the serious rail accidents to date. Howland caused people to sit up and take notice about safety on trains. Before 1840 ended the first crossing signs went up along a railway: The Western Railroad in Massachusetts put up signs that read, LOOK OUT FOR THE ENGINE WHILE THE BELL RINGS.

But despite such new precautions railroad people in those early days seem to have taken accidents as a matter of course. Stories were told during this time about locomotives that would hit people, horses, carriages and wagons—and not even slow down!

The first railroad crossing signs
were put to use in 1840.

The Genius of Matthias Baldwin

During the early 1830s, Matthias William Baldwin was proving to be one of the most important early locomotive makers in the United States. Baldwin, who was a jewelry maker by trade, first became interested in railroading when Benjamin Franklin Peale asked him to build a small locomotive for the Peale Museum in Philadelphia. Peale's father, Charles Willson Peale, had been a famous American painter and scientist. He had painted many portraits of George Washington and other Revolutionary War leaders. During his lifetime he had collected many curious scientific objects and animal skeletons, including some of the first dinosaurs unearthed in the United States. Benjamin Franklin Peale ran the museum that housed this collection after his father died.

Baldwin, who had already built a stationary or non-moving steam engine, agreed to build a special engine for a small railroad that people could ride inside the Peale

Museum. He began work on the "toy train" on April 25, 1831. Baldwin built an engine, two cars and a circular track. Each car would seat four people. When completed, the little railroad became the most popular attraction in the Peale Museum.

Baldwin Builds Old Ironsides

People flocked to the museum from all over Philadelphia to ride the indoor train. Some of the visitors were interested in more than just a train ride. They were part of a business group that wanted to build a rail line connecting Philadelphia, Germantown and Norristown. The railway would run six miles. They asked Baldwin if he would help them build their railroad. He accepted.

To help him design a large locomotive, Baldwin visited the machine shop of the Camden and Amboy Railway. There, mechanics were busy assembling an imported British locomotive. Baldwin observed them and went back to his workshop. In six months, he built a six-ton, full-sized locomotive called Old Ironsides. After testing and trying the locomotive, Baldwin perfected the engine, giving it a speed of 28 miles per hour while pulling 30 tons.

Even after putting Old Ironsides to work, transporting people and produce along the Philadelphia, Germantown and Norristown line, Baldwin continued improving his locomotive. A year later the steam engine ran a mile in a few seconds less than a minute. This was a great speed for a locomotive at that time. Today this famous locomotive can be seen in the Franklin Institute Museum in Philadelphia.

Old Ironsides, the famous six-ton, high-speed locomotive designed by Matthias Baldwin

Baldwin Continues His Work

Because of Baldwin's success at building a fast locomotive, other railways asked him to build locomotives for them. Over the next ten years, Baldwin built one locomotive a year, each one improving on the last. Many of the Baldwin engines were used in rail service for as long as 30 years.

Baldwin made important improvements to the steam engine and to railroad technology in general. He built metal joints that would hold more steam pressure. He experimented with using coal for fuel and became the first to burn coal in locomotives. He improved railway wheels, changing the wooden wheels banded with steel to all-steel wheels. In 1842 he patented a locomotive design that helped trains travel around sharp curves. In 1854 Matthias Baldwin founded the Baldwin Locomotive Works. By 1866, the year of his death, his company had made and sold more than 1,500 locomotives.

Changes Through the Years

Many important changes on America's railroads came about in the years between 1830 and 1850. Men like Baldwin improved the engines, the wheels, the rails, the carriages and every other part of rail travel. Some of the changes were made for better safety. Others were made to make trains go faster and run more smoothly. Still others were made to give passengers a more comfortable ride.

From English to American Locomotives

Work on steam locomotives and railroads had begun in Great Britain before any real interest in them developed in the United States. For this reason, the first steam engines came from Britain. In 1831 a British locomotive called the

John Bull No. 1 was put into service on the Camden and Amboy Railway. Another British import found work on the Mohawk and Hudson line. British locomotives were used on railways in Massachusetts, Maryland and other states. Often, when an American railway ordered a British locomotive, British engineers came with it. These workers ran and operated the new engines.

But American railways did not use foreign locomotives or engineers for long. For one thing many of the early British engines were too heavy for American tracks. Some of them weighed over six tons. Often American mechanics would take apart the British models and rebuild them to make lighter locomotives.

One of those mechanics was John B. Jervis, who worked for the Mohawk and Hudson line. While rebuilding English locomotives, Jervis made important changes, including changing single pairs of wheels at the ends of

The President

each car to a truck assembly made of two axles and four wheels, setting the wheels closer together. This change gave the locomotive a shorter wheelbase, which is the difference between the front and rear wheels. It allowed the engine to take curves with less stress exerted on the wheels and rails. This improvement to the wheel system of locomotives helped change the locomotive system for the future. It also led to the development of an American style of locomotive.

The President and the Victoria

It did not take long for carriage designs to change. The Philadelphia, Germantown and Norristown may have been the first American railroad to break away from the stage-coach design for passenger cars. By 1837 the P,G & N was busy trying out the President and the Victoria—two

★

new carriages. Each new car ran on eight wheels rather than four. Both had doors at each end, and the seats ran along the sides with an aisle in the middle. At the end of this new type of car was a little room, like a rest room, about five feet square, for women. In the room at the other end of the car was a bar where men could drink.

These new car designs caught on in a hurry. From the boxy, uncomfortable cars of the early days, passenger cars grew steadily sleeker. Nearly all American railroads would remodel their cars until they came to resemble the passenger cars of this century.

Perhaps there was one notable exception to this design change. For many years the Erie and Kalamazoo Railroad, whose tracks ran from Adrian, Michigan, to Toledo, Ohio, had rail cars that looked like Swiss cuckoo clocks. Each car had two windows below and one above, along with a large, ornamental door.

But most other lines patterned their coaches after the Victoria and the President. The average cars grew to between 35 and 40 feet in length and were about 8 feet wide. The inside of the cars was about 6½ feet high. The seats were barely wide enough for two people. The doors and windows were small.

Since the windows were often nailed shut—to keep engine sparks from flying in—the cars were very hot during the summer. Often they were crowded and foul smelling. In cold weather a small stove provided heat. There were many incidents of train derailments that caused internal fires. Sometimes people died in such fires.

Tickets, Please!

Early in American railroading, passengers bought tickets to ride the train. An average ticket might measure ten-by-five inches and was printed on heavy paper. Some railroads issued tokens, or metal disks, to passengers instead. Other lines used glazed cardboard tickets in different colors.

Most of the early success of American railroads came from transporting people, not goods. For example, in 1835 the amount of money paid to railroads in Maryland for hauling goods or freight increased by $8,400. But during the same year in Maryland, receipts for passenger service went up by $148,000.

That year in South Carolina, the Charleston and Hamburg Railroad carried 2,500 people a month in the first six months of the year. This compares to the number of people who traveled this same distance in all the time before the railroad was built. At that time only one stagecoach was needed. It made three trips a week. The numbers of passengers traveling by stage between the towns of Charleston and Hamburg were as few as 50. Certainly many more people were willing to ride the new trains.

Flags and Whistles…and Cab Designs

The earliest trains used a system of flags to signal when the crew should apply the brakes on each car. Often an engineer would hang a flag on a pole to signal that the engine was braking. A crewman, sitting on top of a rail coach, would see the flag and call to the other crewmen to apply the brakes in the other cars. Flag signaling was soon replaced by a steam-generated signal. Engineers opened up steam valves on their engines to let the "hiss" of escaping steam signal all stops. But it took an Englishman named George Stephenson to invent the steam whistle. Soon afterward all American trains used whistles for signaling.

No one knows who invented the typical locomotive **cab**. The cab—short for "cabin"—is the part of the locomotive that houses the engineer and operating controls. The "classic cab" design that most people picture when they think of 19th-century railroad engines was meant to protect engineers from the cold winter winds. The earliest cabs were covered with canvas that could be removed during warm weather. Wooden cabs followed soon after.

Traveling by Night

In the early days of the railroads night travel was unnecessary because all the lines were short enough to travel in one day. But during the 1840s, as the lines grew longer, distances traveled were too long to be made in a single day. Some rails began night runs. At first, most railroads that offered night runs carried only freight, leaving passenger service for the daytime. The Charleston and Hamburg line in South Carolina was one of the first lines to pioneer night service.

Traveling by train at night was, however, very difficult. People had to sleep in the uncomfortable seats. Men would prop up their legs on the seat in front of them and slouch down. But women, not to appear unladylike, had to sit up and sleep. Two candles lighted the car, one at each end of the carriage.

Actually sleeping onboard could be quite a feat. Most of the early trains snapped and jerked as they traveled. Cars were often connected by as much as three feet of chain. Such a distance caused the cars to jerk, especially when the train started and stopped. Most engineers liked to start up their trains by opening the throttle all the way. This action caused the cars to snap into a line with a loud bang. It was common that every man in a passenger car would lose his hat when a train was snapped into high speed.

Perhaps the first headlight for a locomotive in

The invention of the headlight made travel by night possible for America's early railroad systems.

★

31

America was provided by an engineer named Horatio Allen. He connected a small flatcar to the front of the engine. He had the car filled with sand and lit a fire of pine knots on it. The "fire-car" was pushed by the engine and lit the tracks up ahead. The effect was rather eerie, for the fire gave the tracks a spooky, flickering light.

By 1840 engineers were using a more sophisticated method. A kerosene-burning headlight with polished reflectors brightened the night, sending out a steady beam of light.

Traffic Problems on the Railroads

As more and more trains began to travel the rail lines of the United States, traffic problems soon developed. All early rail lines operated on a single set of tracks. But with more trains, the need for trains to pass each other would have to be addressed. Sidetracks, called turnouts, were invented. These sidetracks let a train leave the main track so that another train coming from the opposite direction could pass. But which train would have to leave the main track? Obviously both trains were in a hurry.

To solve the problem, rail lines placed large poles exactly halfway between all turnouts along a route. This pole was called the center pole. Whenever two trains met along a single line of track, the train that passed the center pole first was given the right-of-way. This meant that the train without the right-of-way would have to back up to the nearest turnout and allow the other train to pass.

The early railroad crews were quite competitive, so some trains had head-on collisions racing to beat the other to the center pole. Sometimes different train crews got into fist fights, each claiming they were closer to the turnout than the other. In some of these fights even the passengers got involved!

★

The solution to the traffic problem, railroad officials decided, was to schedule trains on regular runs. So the **timetable**, or train schedule, was born. First called "arrangements of trains," early timetables were very inaccurate. Trains rarely arrived or departed according to the timetable. In these early days of the railroad, trains basically arrived at stations when they *could*, not when they were expected.

To help give waiting passengers some idea of when to expect a train, wooden towers were built at stations. Station agents would climb up these towers as soon as a train was "expected." Using a **spyglass**, the agent would scout the horizon for the engine's smoke and trail. The moment he saw any sign of the distant locomotive, the agent would climb down and tell the people at the station that the train would be arriving soon. Sometimes the agent would ring a bell or blow a horn when he spied the oncoming train.

Adopting the Standard Gauge

As early rail lines grew and began to come closer and closer to each other, the problem of track gauge became important. **Gauge** refers to the distance between the rails on a track. When the rail lines were first built, the gauges varied. This meant that different rail lines could not be connected with each other because the track width was not the same. For example, the Baltimore and Ohio line was built with a 4-foot 8-inch gauge. Railroads in Maryland and Pennsylvania used the same gauge. But other lines used different gauges. The Charleston and Hamburg used a gauge of 5 feet. The Camden and Amboy used 4 feet 10 inches. Some gauges ran as wide as six feet. It was not until the 1870s that nearly all American railroads had switched to the standard British gauge of 4 feet 8½ inches.

★

Keeping Cattle in Their Place

In the farmlands that the early railroads passed through, horses and cows had a habit of wandering onto the tracks. When the Camden and Amboy line faced this problem, head mechanic Isaac Dripps came up with an interesting invention: the cowcatcher. Dripps built a short, metal, wedge-shaped contraption that he attached to the front of the engine. It had several pointed iron bars sticking out in front of the engine. The idea was to catch any animal on the tracks and keep it from sliding under the locomotive's wheels.

The idea worked. Just days after attaching the first cowcatcher to a locomotive, the train hit a rather large bull. But the cowcatcher worked too well. The pointed iron bars pierced the animal, killing it. The train was stopped, and men had to pull the bull off the iron spikes. Soon the cowcatcher was changed so that it would simply push an animal off the tracks.

Grasshoppers and the Railroads

In 1836 a plague of grasshoppers darkened the skies over Pennsylvania. Billions of the creatures filled farmlands and fields. They littered the railroad tracks, causing problems as the trains ran over them. Their squashed bodies greased the tracks, making engine wheels slip and slide, so that the train was unable to gain speed. At first armies of men used brooms to sweep the grasshoppers from the tracks. But this took a long time and the insects were back on the tracks again when the next train came along. Brooms were then mounted on the fronts of locomotives. But the brooms fell apart quickly with all that sweeping.

Then someone decided to use sand to help the trains gain traction. A box of dry sand was mounted on top of the engine, with pipes running down the sides of the locomotive to points in front of the wheels. The sand gave the train wheels something to ride on other than grasshopper bodies. In fact, after the plague of grasshoppers was over, railroads continued to use sand for better traction for decades to come.

Building Fancy Locomotives

For the most part early locomotives were built to do a particular job. In the 1830s engine designers were concerned only with how well the locomotive worked. No one cared much about dressing them up.

But by the late 1840s, and for the next 30 years, locomotive builders went to great lengths to make their engines look more attractive. These builders wanted their trains to look good on the tracks as they sped from town to town. The Taunton Locomotive Works of Massachusetts became a leader in train decorating. Many of the locomotives built by this company in the years between 1847 and 1870 had the running gear painted several different colors. Inside, the engine cab was lined with mahogany or walnut paneling, and the engineer's seat was nicely upholstered.

Many of Matthias Baldwin's locomotives were also decorated. One named Tiger, built in 1857, was a wild combination of colors. The smokestack, **firebox** and the engine or steam dome above the boiler were painted black. The wheels and cowcatcher were painted bright red. The tender was a light rose shade, while the boiler was a robin's egg blue. On the outside of the cab a Bengal tiger had been painted against a deep green jungle background. The name of the railroad company was painted on the side of the tender in fancy lettering. And to give the locomotive a truly patriotic look, the American flag flew from a bronze mast on top of the cowcatcher.

★

Improvements from the Ground Up

Improvements to railroading came fast. Early rail lines were made of wood with iron straps used to attach the rails to the wooden ties. This system proved very inefficient. Robert L. Stevens, who worked for the Camden and Amboy line, developed a kind of track that would replace the wooden rails of the early train system. Stevens first carved his new design out of wood. Then it was forged in steel. The result was the T-shaped rail that railroads still use today.

★

The Tiger was one of Baldwin's most decorated locomotives.

These rails worked well with the new "**friction wheel**," invented by Ross Winans, a mechanic from the B & O Railroad. The friction wheel had a lip so that it could ride comfortably on the T-rail.

The Illinois Central

Rails West to the Mississippi

B y 1837 about 200 railroads were either in use or being built, planned or dreamed about. Most of those rail lines would eventually be built. Private companies and state governments sank millions of dollars into railroad expansion. The first successful lines, like the Camden and Amboy, the Baltimore and Ohio and the Charleston and Hamburg helped railroad service gain acceptance across the United States. During the 1850s railroad builders looked west for further expansion.

One of the first states they eyed was Illinois. As early as 1837, Illinois had voted to begin a program of canal, road and railroad building. However, Illinois's plans were halted when the United States economy went through a depression. During the next 14 years state leaders pushed to get a railroad charter from the Illinois government. Finally, in 1851 the state granted a charter to the Illinois Central Railroad Company. This new corporation

★

was different from almost all others, because with the charter came land— lots of land. The Illinois Central obtained a **land grant** of over 2.5 million acres of public land. A look at the early years of the Illinois Central reveals how such a railroad helped bring people and prosperity to this midwestern state. It also shows how, in the 1850s, the coming of a railroad could change the shape of westward migration and settlement.

Laying Out the Lines

Under the Illinois Central (IC) charter the new railroad agreed to build 700 miles of track in six years. The railroad also agreed to pay the state 7 percent of the line's gross profit. The company was to raise money to build the railroad by selling land from its 2.5 million acres. The charter also required the IC to build 50 miles of track in two years. The main line was to be finished in four years, and all branch lines completed in six years.

The main line of the IC would run from the Wisconsin border through the middle of Illinois, south to Cairo, where the Mississippi and Ohio rivers come together. The branch line was to run from Centralia, in southern Illinois, to Chicago, the railroad **terminus**. When the 700 miles were finished, the IC would be the longest railroad in America.

Immigrants Help Build the Lines

Before the IC could begin building, the company needed workers. Because so many other railroads were being built at that time, it was hard to get workers to come to Illinois. Many of the people who worked for the railroads in the 1850s were Irish and German immigrants. IC's chief engineer, Roswell Mason, hired men to go to New York City, where so many of the new immigrants had settled, to

★

Thousands of immigrants were put to work
building the Illinois Central Railroad.

find railroad workers. The IC ran ads in the local newspapers. But by the spring of 1853, the IC had only 3,000 men to build the rail line. It needed twice that number.

Mason then worked out a poster campaign to attract workers to Illinois. He had thousands of posters printed and placed all over New York City. The posters said the IC needed 3,000 rail workers. Anyone who would travel to Illinois would be paid $1.25 a day and promised steady work for two years. The posters worked. After that the IC always had plenty of workers. Sometimes the rail line had as many as 10,000 workers at one time.

By September 1856 the main line and the branch lines of the Illinois Central were completed. They were finished ahead of schedule. It was the longest single railroad line in the United States. There were hundreds of celebrations along the line. Most of the parties, picnics and barbecues were held when the first train came through each of the little towns along the line. Wagons full of people came from the country to see the first IC locomotives.

The IC Brings People West

The first railroads in America were built in the East, in areas where many people already lived. But that was not the case in Illinois. The Illinois government had done little to attract settlers to its lands. The IC changed all of this when it began selling off much of the land it owned along its tracks. The land was sold to farmers and immigrants who wanted to start new lives. The IC knew that it would need to sell land to thousands of newcomers to raise enough money.

The IC designed fancy posters and handbills to give to people back East. The posters painted a very pretty and tempting picture of what life in Illinois could be like. The prices of the IC lands were very reasonable. Over 100,000

★

Posters like this one, designed by the IC, were used to increase the population of Illinois and attract workers to the railroad.

of the posters were mailed to eastern and southern farmers. Others went up on post office walls.

Advertisements were run in many of the large eastern newspapers, offering land to immigrants and farmers. All this advertising did the job. Many people decided to move west to Illinois. The population of the state doubled from 851,000 in 1850 to more than 1,700,000 in 1860. Another 600,000 people moved to Illinois during the 1860s. But the railroad was not only responsible for bringing new settlers to the state. It also decided where important cities would be located by its choice of where railway stations would be built along the route.

★

Today's railroads continue to be an important part of America's transportation system.

★

44

The Growth of the Railroads

During the 1830s, 1840s and 1850s, railroads became the most widely used form of transportation in the United States. Never had a means of carrying freight and people caught on so quickly and become so popular. During this same period many canals were being built as well. And steamboats were popular on American rivers. But it was the railroads that swept the country.

By 1840 there were nearly 2,000 miles of track in use in America. A decade later more than 9,000 miles of track had been built. In that same year, 1850, all but a few hundred of the 9,000 miles of track could be found along the eastern seaboard and adjoining states.

But by 1856 in Ohio, for example, there were over 2,500 miles of railroads in operation, with another 2,000 still being built. Ohio's western neighbor, Indiana, had nearly 1,300 miles in use and nearly 1,600 under construction.

★

When the Civil War broke out in 1861, the state of Illinois had almost 3,000 miles of railroad track in use and the great city of Chicago could boast of 11 different rail lines that ran into it. By the end of the Civil War, railroads crisscrossed several states west of the Mississippi, with 3,300 miles of track in use. Most of these lines ran through Missouri, Texas and Iowa. At that same time the total miles of track east of the Mississippi River came to nearly 32,000. Today trains are used and relied upon by people everywhere. With the inventions and improvements that have taken place during the past 200 years, railroads have managed to find a permanent place in America's transportation system.

For Further Reading

Harvey, T. *Railroads*. Minneapolis: Lerner Publications, 1980.

Holbrook, Suzanne. *Faster Than a Horse*. Louisville, KY: Westminster Press, 1983.

Jefferis, David. *Trains: The History of Railroads*. New York: Franklin Watts, Inc., 1991.

Kanetzke, Howard W. *Trains and Railroads*. Milwaukee: Raintree Publishers, 1987.

Miller, Marilyn. *The Trans-Continental Railroad*. Morristown, NJ: Silver Burdett Press, 1985.

Steele, Philip. *Trains*. New York: Crestwood House, 1991.

Glossary

barrier car—A flat car, piled with cotton bales, and placed between the steam locomotive and the passenger carriages. Served to protect passengers from explosions.

cab—The part of a locomotive that houses the engineer and the operating controls.

charter—A legal document giving someone official permission to do something such as build railroads in a state.

firebox—A chamber that contains a fire, as in a furnace or steam boiler.

friction wheel—A type of railroad car wheel that had a lip or flange on the inside so that it could comfortably fit on a T-rail.

gauge—The distance or width between two rails.

land grant—A grant or gift of land made by the government especially for roads, railroads or agricultural colleges.

locomotive—A self-propelled vehicle that runs on rails.

machine shop—A workshop in which metal parts are made to size and assembled for machine use.

safety valve—An automatic escape or relief valve used on a steam boiler. This allows the steam pressure to escape, thus avoiding an explosion.

snake head—A loose railroad tie. Early ties were tied down to the rail bed by straps. When a strap broke, the tie might stick up, causing a hazard to approaching rail cars.

spyglass—A small telescope that was similar to today's binoculars but designed for single-eye viewing.

steam boiler—A boiler for producing steam.

steam engine—An engine driven by steam.

switch—A device made of two movable rails and necessary connections. It was designed to turn a locomotive or train from one track to another.

terminus—Either end of a transportation line or travel route.

tie—One of the wooden supports used in a railroad bed. Rails were spiked or strapped to these.

timetable—A schedule of arrivals and departures for trains.

turntable—A revolving platform with a track for turning wheeled vehicles, such as locomotives.

Index

★